my friendly neighborhood

Librarian

Published in the United States of America by Cherry Lake Publishing
Ann Arbor, Michigan
www.cherrylakepublishing.com

Reading Adviser: Marla Conn MS, Ed., Literacy specialist, Read-Ability, Inc.
Book Design: Jennifer Wahi
Illustrator: Jeff Bane

Photo Credits: © Lisa F. Young / Shutterstock.com, 5; © Liderina / Shutterstock.com, 7; © wavebreakmedia / Shutterstock.com, 9, 15, 17, 21; © Comaniciu Dan / Shutterstock.com, 11; © Monkey Business Images / Shutterstock.com, 13; © Jasminko Ibrakovic / Shutterstock.com, 19; © Tyler Olson / Shutterstock.com, 23; © aleksandr-mansurov-ru, 2-3, 24; Cover, 1, 10, 12, 16, Jeff Bane

Library of Congress Cataloging-in-Publication Data has been filed and is available at catalog.loc.gov

Printed in the United States of America
Corporate Graphics

table of contents

About the author: Samantha Bell has written and illustrated over 60 books for children. She lives in South Carolina with her family and pets. She is very thankful for the helpers in her community.

About the illustrator: Jeff Bane and his two business partners own a studio along the American River in Folsom, California, home of the 1849 Gold Rush. When Jeff's not sketching or illustrating for clients, he's either swimming or kayaking in the river to relax.

neighborhood helper

Many people visit the library.
They need **information**.
Librarians help them find it.

Librarians know where to look.
They look in new and old books.
They use computers.

Some people want books to read. Some want sad books. Some want scary books. Librarians help people find books.

What kinds of books do you like to read?

Some librarians work in **public** libraries. They help everyone.

THE NEW YORK PUBLIC LIBRARY
THE ASTOR LIBRARY
THE LENOX LIBRARY
THE TILDEN TRUST
BOOKS AT NOON
Fifth Ave
public eye
175 Years of Sharing Photography
FREE EXHIBITION

They show people how to use computers. They set up classes.

Some plan events for children.
They plan story times.

Some help students do **research**.

What do you need help with?

Some librarians work in **colleges**. They help college students.

Some librarians work in schools. They help students. They help teachers.

Librarians love to read. They want us to love to read, too.

What would you like to ask a librarian?

glossary & index

glossary

colleges (KAH-lih-jiz) places of higher learning where students can continue to study after finishing high school

information (in-fur-MAY-shuhn) facts and knowledge you get by searching or by listening

public (PUHB-lik) something for all the people in the community

research (REE-surch) careful study about something that requires collecting information

index